TOGG AND LEFTOVER IN TROUBLE

Mike Ratnett and June Goulding

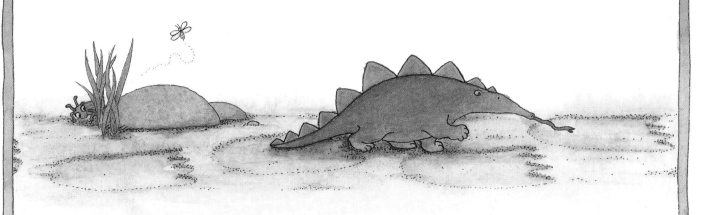

PictureLions

An Imprint of HarperCollins*Publishers*

For Lucy, Gary and Adam

First published in Great Britain by HarperCollins Publishers Ltd in 1992
First published in Picture Lions in 1993
Picture Lions is an imprint of the Children's Division, part of HarperCollins Publishers Limited,
77-85 Fulham Palace Road, Hammersmith, London W6 8JB

ISBN 0 00 664296-9

Printed in Great Britain by BPCC Paulton Books

This book is set in Americana

One morning, Togg and Leftover got up very early.

"Come on, sleepyhead," said Togg. "Today is Flowulf's birthday, and if we don't hurry they'll start the party without us!"

Leftover nodded excitedly.

"It's going to be a wonderful party," said Togg. "Everyone's invited except for those mischievous cavepeople across the river. They always spoil things."

The sun was still rising as the friends reached their special bathing pool.

"No splashing today!" said Togg.

"*KERSPLASH!*" went Leftover.
"Eek!" Togg squealed. "It's freezing!"

While Togg dried himself, Leftover picked some flowers.
"That's a good idea," said Togg. "Flowulf will like those."

But when Togg and Leftover arrived at the party an awful sight met them.

"That dinosaur's got a cheek coming back here!" said Redbeard. "Look what he's done! He's wrecked our party."

"Yes," said Flowulf. "He came charging through here this morning and he's ruined everything."

"He couldn't have," said Togg. "He's been with me all the time. Anyway, you'd never do something like this, would you, Leftover?"

But though the dinosaur shook his head and looked very sad, nobody believed him.

"We all saw him," said Coppertop. "And look! Who else has footprints that big?"

And there in the sand were lots of giant footprints that looked just like Leftover's.

"Now we're going to tidy up and have our party without you," said Redbeard. "So goodbye!"

Poor Togg and Leftover were very sad as they trudged away – so sad that they didn't notice they were being watched.

"Oh dear," sighed Togg. "I just don't understand it.
Then he had an idea.
  "I know," he said. "Let's follow the footprints to find out!"
  And they set off together.

The footprints led Togg and Leftover up and down, and around and around, until they ended at a secret, bushy place.

"Shhh," said Togg. "I can hear voices."

And they stopped and listened. And as they listened their eyes grew wide.

"So that's what happened," whispered Togg.

And they crept away.

That afternoon, Togg's friends were right in the middle of their party when it happened again.

"Help!" screamed the cavepeople. "It's Leftover. He's come back!"

And a moment later a huge dinosaur came thundering through, knocking tables everywhere, while the cavepeople fled before him.

But then they stared in amazement. For there, charging towards the first dinosaur from the opposite direction, was a second dinosaur.

"*Gallumph, gallumph, gallumph, gallumph!*"

"Crash!" went the dinosaurs as they ran into each other and the first dinosaur's legs went limp and wobbly.

"Bash!" went the dinosaurs and the first dinosaur fell to pieces, tumbling cavepeople everywhere.

"It's those cavepeople from across the river!" said Redbeard.
   "Yes," said Togg. "Leftover and I followed the footprints and heard them plotting to come back."
   "After them everyone!" said Coppertop.
   And they chased the mischief makers right out of sight.

"We're really sorry we thought it was you, Leftover," said Flowulf.

"You're a real hero," they said.

"But what can we do now?" said Redbeard. "There's nothing left."

"I know," said Togg. "Let's have a Dinosaur party.

We can use all these bits and pieces to make costumes, and Leftover can be the judge."

So that's just what they did. And Leftover said that Flowulf was the winner and gave her a special dinosaur hug for her prize.

"Did you enjoy yourself, Leftover?" asked Togg as they walked home.

And Leftover nodded. It was fun to give hugs. And very nice being a hero.